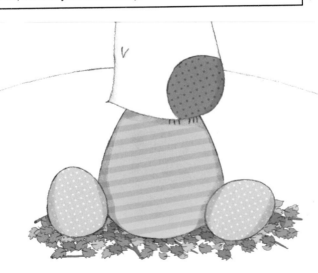

h
Hodder
Children's

For Iain

Text and illustrations copyright © Fiona Roberton 2013

First published by Penguin Group Australia, 250 Camberwell Road, Camberwell, Vic 3124, Australia
First published in the UK in hardback in 2013 by Hodder Children's Books
First published in paperback in 2014

Hodder Children's Books, 338 Euston Road, London, NW1 3BH
Hodder Children's Books Australia, Level 17/207 Kent Street, Sydney, NSW 2000

The right of Fiona Roberton to be identified as the author and illustrator of this Work
has been asserted by her in accordance with the Copyright, Designs and Patents Act 1988.

A catalogue record of this book is available from the British Library.

ISBN 978 1 444 91261 6

Printed in China

Hodder Children's Books is a division of Hachette Children's Books, an Hachette UK Company

www.hachette.co.uk

Cuckoo hatched,

and all was well.

Until the other birds discovered Cuckoo...

...was different.

They couldn't understand
a word Cuckoo was saying,

no matter how
hard Cuckoo tried.

It was all extremely
confusing for everyone.

So Cuckoo decided it would be best
if he left, and bravely went in search of
someone who *could* understand him.

He spotted some sheep in the distance
and flew over to say hello.

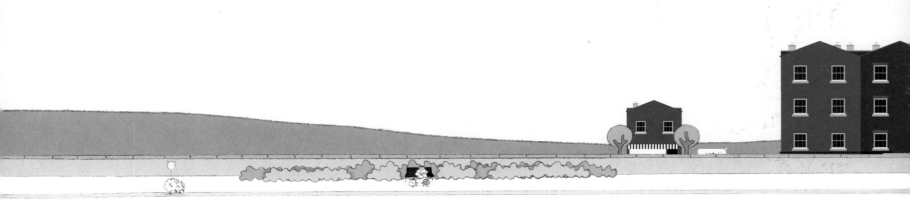

But the sheep couldn't understand him either,

and neither could the frogs,

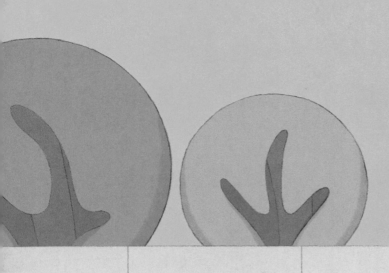

or the pigs,

or the snakes,

or the cows,

or even the rabbits.

CAACKAA!

pat
pat
pat

THUMP!

THUMP!

THUMP!

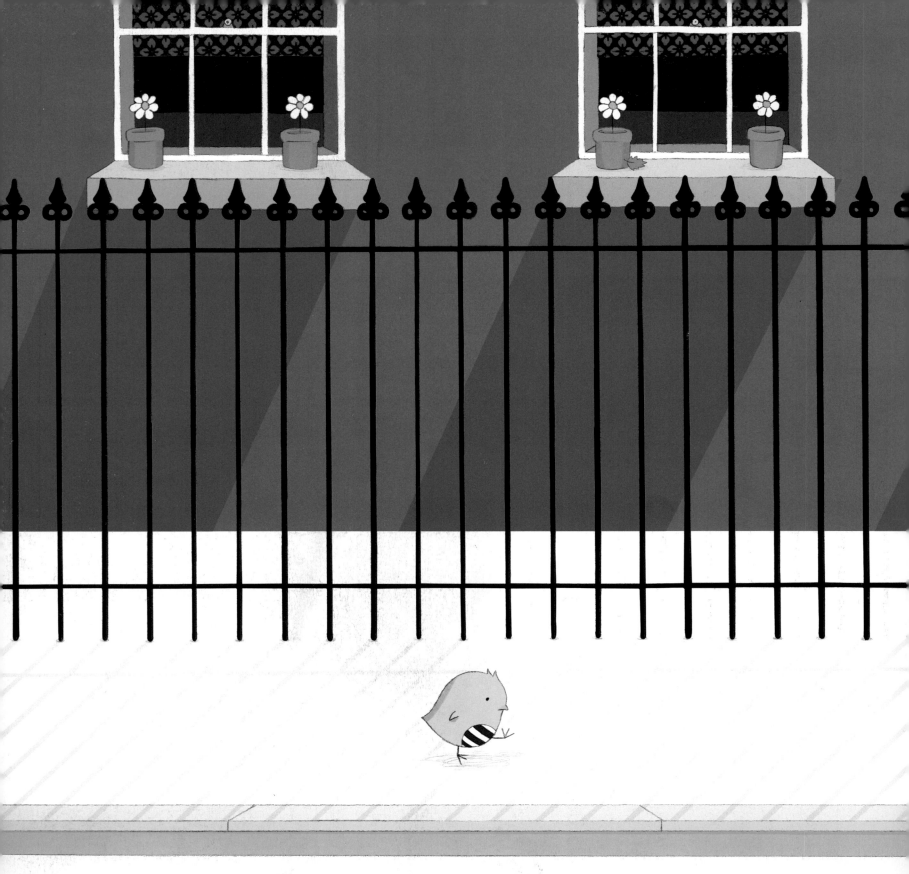

Cuckoo just couldn't seem to find
anyone who spoke his language.

But then Cuckoo had a brilliant idea.
He would learn theirs instead!

But even though Cuckoo tried…

and tried...

Sssssssock!

THUMP!

THUMP!

THUMP!

pat

pat

pat

as hard as he possibly could, he just couldn't get the hang of any of them.

CUMONKSSSSSS BAGRITUUCKOO THUBIITOOOMP!

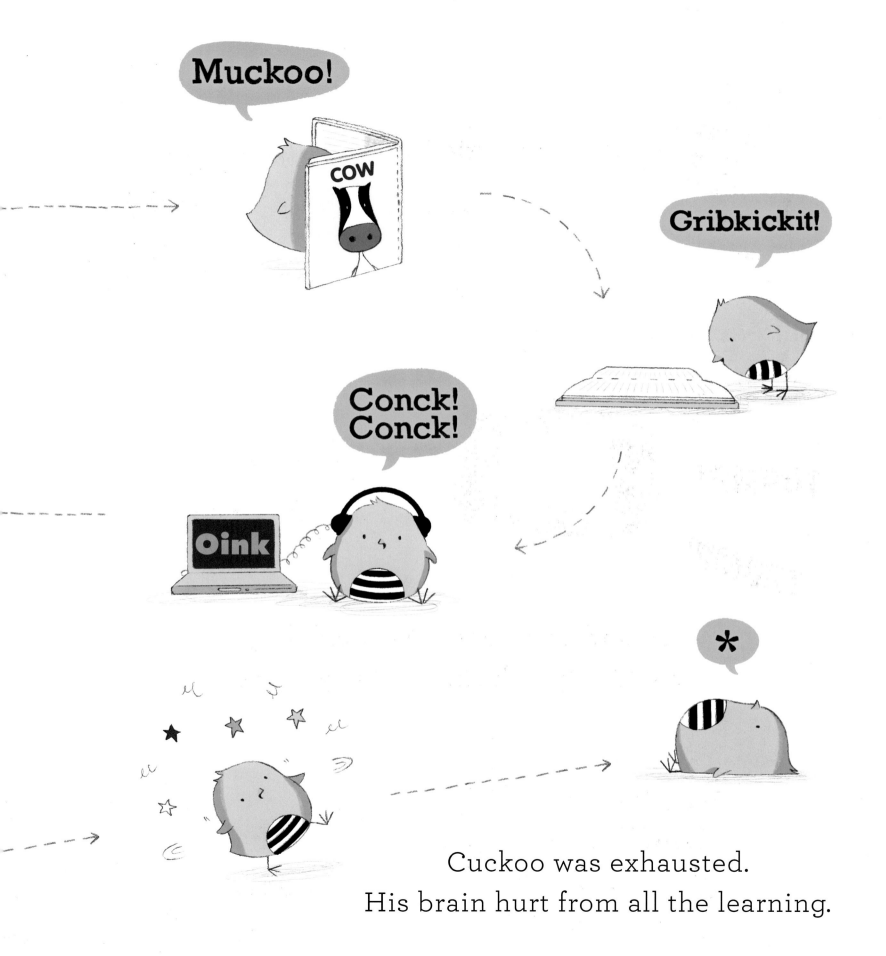

Cuckoo was exhausted.
His brain hurt from all the learning.

He flew up into the rooftops to find a nice warm spot to sleep, and was just about to close his eyes…

...when from out of the twilight,
he thought he heard the faintest...

Cuckoo couldn't believe his ears.
It couldn't be, could it?

Cuckoo raced as fast as his little wings could carry him, from window...

to window...

to window,
until at last...

he finally found...

Cuckoo!

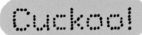

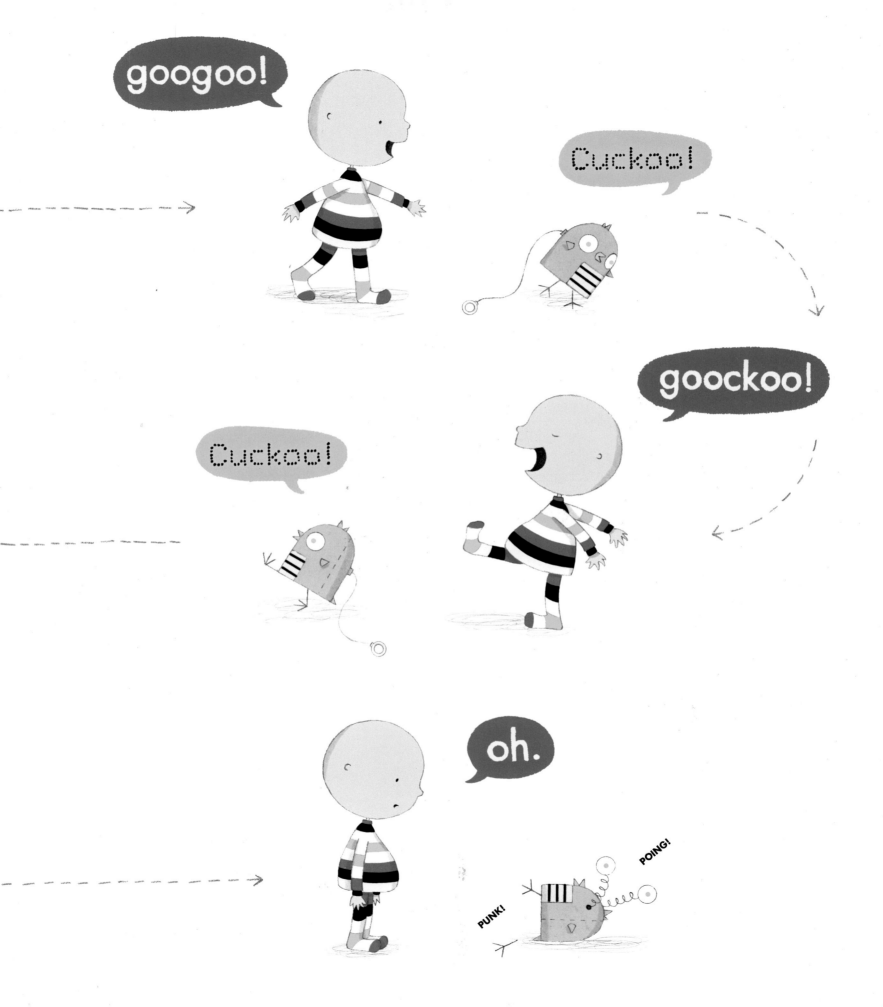

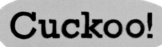

Someone who understood him...

...perfectly.